GIRLS ROCK!

Football Crazy

Shey Kettle

illustrated by
Meredith Thomas

RISING STARS

First published in Great Britain by
RISING STARS UK LTD 2008
22 Grafton Street, London W1S 4EX

For information visit our website at:
www.risingstars-uk.com

British Library Cataloguing in Publication Data
A CIP record for this book is available from the British Library.

ISBN: 978 1 84680 268 3

First published in 2008 by
MACMILLAN EDUCATION AUSTRALIA PTY LTD
15–19 Claremont Street, South Yarra 3141

Visit our website at www.macmillan.com.au

Associated companies and representatives throughout the world.

Copyright © Felice Arena, Phil Kettle and Shey Kettle 2008

Series created by Felice Arena and Phil Kettle
Project management by Limelight Publishing Services Pty Ltd
Cover and text design by Lore Foye
Illustrations by Meredith Thomas

Printed in China

GIRLS ROCK!
Contents

Carly   *Mai*

CHAPTER 1

The Weekend at Last!

Mai and Carly are walking home from school together. They're both really excited because it's Friday. And everyone knows that Friday means two things—the school week has finished and the weekend has started.

Mai "I love weekends."

Carly "Yeah, so do I."

Mai "So, what are we going to do?"

Carly "I think we should practise our football skills."

Mai "Why?"

Carly "'Cause I watched the school football team train today and I want to be on the team."

Mai "But there are only boys on the school football team."

Carly "So? I think we're as good as them, and I think we should be on the team too!"

Mai "Yeah, but they probably won't let us be on the team."

Carly "Well, I think if we're good enough, they'll just have to let us."

Mai (laughing) "I think we'd need to be better than all of them, maybe even as good as Beckham."

Carly "Come on Mai, we should try. I know that I'm as good as they are—maybe even better!"

Mai "Okay! If you're game to try out for the team, then so am I."

Carly "Right. Let's start now. We can practise our passing with this can."

Carly and Mai take it in turns to kick an empty drink can they find on the footpath. They kick it to each other, as if it were a football. The girls stop when they come to the park.

Carly "Hey! This is where we should come and practise."

Mai "What about the Hoover boys next door?"

Carly "You mean Joel and Jarred Hoover Vacuum-Cleaner? What about them?"

Mai "Well, we don't want them to come and play while we're here."

Carly "I'll just tell them that we've come to give them a big fat kiss— that'll soon scare them off."

Mai and Carly laugh.

Mai "What'll we wear?

Carly "Let's borrow football kits from our brothers. They're not playing a game tomorrow."

Mai "Great idea. Let's not tell them though, or they might laugh at us."

The girls agree to meet the next morning.

CHAPTER 2

Looking Good

Mai and Carly arrive at the park at nine o'clock the next morning. Both girls are dressed in football kits they've secretly taken from their brothers' wardrobes.

Mai "Wow! You look just like a professional player."

Carly "So do you!"

Mai "If the school coach could see us he'd put us on the team right now."

Carly (laughing) "I think that he'd want to see us play first."

Mai "Well, we should start training."

Carly "Great idea, but we're missing something."

Mai "What?"

Carly "A football."

Mai "I thought you had one."

Carly "Well, I thought you had one."

Mai "So, we look like real players, we talk like real players—but we haven't got a football."

Mai "Maybe we just pretend that we're kicking and heading a ball."

Carly "I think we need to train with a proper ball if we're going to be good enough to get on the school team."

Mai "Yeah, you're right."

Carly "Any ideas?"

Mai "I know what we can do."

Carly "What?"

Mai "We can go next door and ask the Hoover boys if we can use their football."

Carly "But if we do that, then they'll know we're playing here, and what's worse, they might want to play."

Carly and Mai sit on the ground
looking at each other, until Mai
jumps up.

Mai "I've got a plan!"
Carly "What? What's your plan?"
Mai "Well, first I've got to run home
 and get something. You wait here."

Mai runs home as fast as she can.

CHAPTER 3

Trust Me!

In a couple of minutes Mai returns holding something small in her hand.

Carly "So, what have you got there?"

Mai "I've got something that will make sure that the Hoover boys won't want to play football with us."

Carly "What? Show me. Come on, show me."

Mai "Shut your eyes and I'm going to put it on you. And when I do, I'm sure those Hoover boys won't want to come near us."

Carly hesitates, then shrugs her shoulders and shuts her eyes.

Carly "I hope you know what you're doing."

Mai "Trust me."

Carly "That's what you said when I asked you not to tell Joel Hoover that I liked him."

Mai "He forced me to tell."

Carly "Yeah, right!"

Carly shuts her eyes. Mai uses a red lipstick to cover Carly's face with little red dots. Soon Carly looks like she has a really bad red-spot disease.

Mai "Now we can go and ask the Hoover boys for a loan of their football, 'cause when they see your face, there's no way they'll want to come and play with us in the park."

Carly "Great, but I don't want to ask them unless I can put lipstick dots on your face, too."

Mai agrees. Soon, Carly stands back and admires her handiwork.

Carly "Okay, now we're good. Let's go and ask them for the ball."

CHAPTER 4

Red-spot Disease

The girls knock on the Hoover boys'
door. They hear a vacuum cleaner being
turned off. When Joel Hoover opens the
door, he steps backwards quickly and
trips over the vacuum cleaner. He tells
the girls not to come any closer.

Carly "Hey, Joel, you look like you've just seen a ghost."

Mai "Yeah Joel, haven't you ever seen anyone with the very contagious red-spot disease before?"

Carly "Don't worry, we won't come too close, because if we breathe on you, you'll get the same bad red-spot disease."

Mai "And if you get the same disease as us, then you won't be able to play in the school football team."

Carly "So there!"

Mai "All we want is to borrow your football."

Carly "Yeah! And if you don't let us use your football, we might have to breathe all over you."

Keeping his distance, Joel throws his football to the girls. He tells them that they'll never be any good at football because they are girls.

Carly "You haven't seen us play. We're better than you and your brother. We could beat you any day."

Mai "Yeah! We could beat you, even with the bad red-spot disease."

The girls go back to the park and start kicking and heading the football.

Mai "Hey, I think that football is a pretty easy game. All you've got to do is kick the ball."

Carly "Yeah! Watch me, I bet I can kick the ball from one end of the park to the other."

Carly kicks the ball. It really does go from one end of the park to the other.

Mai "Now watch me! I'm going to dribble!"

Carly (giggling) "Boys are really good at dribbling. Ha! Mostly down the front of their shirts."

Mai "And here come the two best dribblers ever!"

CHAPTER 5

We're the Best

Joel and his brother Jarred are walking towards the girls. They're dressed in their football kits, but they look like they've come from outer space.

Carly (laughing) "So what do you two think you're doing?"

Mai "And why are you wearing those underwater masks and snorkels?"

The boys mumble that they want to play football, but they don't want to catch the red-spot disease.

Carly "Well, I think that we can play a game with you, as long as you keep wearing those masks."

Mai "Yeah, but only if you promise that if we beat you, you won't laugh when we try out for the school football team."

The boys nod in agreement.

Carly "Let's have a goal kick-off. Whoever misses first, loses."

Mai "Great idea! We go first because we're sick, and because we're girls."

The girls move two rubbish bins to mark off a goal area.

Carly "I'll go first."

Carly puts the football on the ground and then runs and kicks it as hard as she can. The football flies between the bins. The girls jump up and down with excitement.

Mai "Great kick! We're one up. It's your turn, Hoover boys."

Jarred lines the ball up to take his kick. He moves in to kick and then stops and mumbles something.

Mai (looking at Carly) "What's he trying to say?"

Carly "Not sure, but I think his goggles have fogged up. Maybe he can't see anything."

Mai "Hey, Jarred, that's bad luck about your goggles fogging up. But if you don't take your kick, then we're the winners."

Carly "And if you miss the goal, guess what? We win anyway!"

Joel mumbles about having girls on the school football team. Jarred runs at the ball and kicks. The football zooms though the air, missing the goal, and over the fence into the boys' backyard.

Carly "Wow, look at it go!"
Mai "Pity it missed the goal."

Mai and Carly roll around laughing.

Carly "So boys, you lost! We won! We're the champions and you're the losers—and now you don't get to laugh when we try out for the school football team on Monday."

Mai "We'll see you later then. It's time for us to go home and wash the lipstick off our faces."

Carly "And don't forget to finish the vacuuming and to take your football inside from your back garden."

Mai "So, boys, we look forward to seeing you at football training next week."

Carly "And don't forget—Girls Rock at football!"

GIRLS ROCK!
Football Lingo

dodging When one player moves quickly away from another player. If you are a good dodger, players in the other team will find it hard to keep up with you.

dribble To move the ball along the ground by running and kicking it to yourself.

goalkeeper The person who tries to stop the other team from getting goals.

header When a player uses their head to pass the ball to another player or to have a shot at a goal.

high five When a player slaps the open hand of their team mates, especially to celebrate scoring a goal.

GIRLS ROCK!
Football Must-dos

☆ Check that your boots have studs—
   you don't want slip over when you're
   running or trying to kick the ball.

☆ Clean your football boots before
   you play. You'll always play better
   in clean football boots. And if you
   don't, at least you'll look a lot better.

☆ Make sure you wear a hair tie if you
   have long hair. There is nothing worse
   than trying to kick the ball when your
   hair is in front of your eyes.

☆ If you want to be a really good
   football player then you have to eat
   healthy food, and do regular training.
   Remember, if you keep on training,
   you'll play better football.

☆ Make sure that you always watch the ball when you are kicking it.

☆ Always shake the hands of the opposing team before the game starts and after the game finishes. And if you win, smile a lot.

☆ Learn to kick the football with both feet. It will help make you a really good player.

☆ Never talk back to the referee. If you do, you might end up getting a penalty for your team.

☆ And remember the most important rule in playing sport is "Make sure you always enjoy the game".

GIRLS ROCK!
Football Instant Info

Football came from England. It is now played in more countries around the world than any other team sport.

The first international game of football was played between Scotland and England in 1872. The score was 0–0.

Football is played on a rectangular field with a goal area and net at each end.

You score a goal in football by kicking or heading the ball over your opponents' goal line at the end of the field.

In football, each goal you score is worth one point.

A football team has eleven players.

The goalkeeper is the only player who is allowed to touch the ball with their hands.

David Beckham is a world-famous English football player.

The emblem for the England football team is three lions.

GIRLS ROCK!
Think Tank

1 Can anyone play on a football team?

2 How many players in a football team?

3 If a football player dribbles, does that mean he or she moves the football with their feet or that they dribble down the front of their shirt?

4 Are goalkeepers allowed to touch the ball with their hands?

5 Who's the best at football, Australia or England?

6 How many points do you score if you get a goal?

7 Is David Beckham a football player or a singer?

8 If you head the ball into the goal, do you score a goal?

Answers

1 Yes! Anyone who is good enough at football can play on a team.

2 There are eleven players in a football team.

3 It means both, but probably in a football game it means he or she moves the ball with their feet.

4 Yes. Goalkeepers are allowed to touch the ball with their hands.

5 England is the best at football, of course!

6 You score one point if you score a goal.

7 A football player … but apparently he sings really well in the shower!

8 Yes, if you head the ball into the goal it counts as a goal.

How did you score?

- If you got all 8 answers correct, then maybe you should be playing football for your country.

- If you got 6 answers correct, you might need to do some more training before trying out for a team.

- If you got fewer than 4 answers correct, then maybe you should think of playing another sport altogether.

Hey Girls!

I hope that you had as much fun reading my story as I had writing it. I loved reading and writing stories when I was young. And in the stories that I wrote, I was always better than I actually was in real life. It was great fun!

At school, why don't you use "Football Crazy" as a play, and you and your friends can be the actors. You can dress up in your football kits. Don't forget to bring your football and football boots, and if your school has a stage, you can pretend that it is a football pitch.

So ... have you decided who's going to be Mai and who's going to be Carly? And who's going to kick off? Make sure that you only pretend to kick off, or else you might get into trouble.

Make sure that you take this story home and get someone to read it out loud to you, or even act out the parts with you.

Reading at home is lots of fun and really important!

And remember, Girls Rock!

Sheykettle.

GIRLS ROCK!
When We Were Kids

Shey

Holly

Shey talked to Holly, another *Girls Rock!* author.

Holly "Were you a good football player when you were young?"

Shey "Yeah, I was pretty good."

Holly "Did you like heading the ball?"

Shey "No, heading the ball can hurt your head."

Holly "So, what were you best at when playing football?"

Shey "I was a great kicker."

Holly "How great?"

Shey "I once kicked a ball 10 kilometres."

Holly "Wow! How did you do that?"

Shey "It was good luck! I kicked the ball and it went over the fence and landed in the back of a moving truck."

GIRLS ROCK!
What a Laugh!

Q Why did the football quit the team?

A Because it got sick of being kicked around!

GIRLS ROCK!

Read about the fun
that girls have in these
GIRLS ROCK! titles:

Birthday Party Blues
Pony Club

Doubles Trouble
Football Crazy

Dance Fever
Minigolf Face-off

Trapeze Dreams
Two at the Zoo

... and 20 more great
titles to choose from!

GIRLS ROCK! books are
available from most booksellers.
For mail order information please
call Rising Stars on 0871 47 23 010
or visit www.risingstars-uk.com